The Northern Lights

Written by
Alice Hemming

Contents

Introduction	4
What are the Northern lights?	6
Why do they appear?	8
Where can you see the Northern lights?	10
When can you see the Northern lights?	12
Stories and science	14

Introduction

These pictures are real photographs of the sky. It looks as if someone has been painting the night sky. The colours seem to mix and dance in the sky.

Are these lights fireworks? Or are they fires from faraway planets, or visiting aliens?

In fact, they are none of these things. The lights are natural and happen often. We call them the Northern lights.

What are the Northern lights?

The Northern lights can have many different shapes and colours. Pale green and pink are common, but you can see bright red, deep purple, yellow and blue as well.

The Northern lights can be shaped like swirls, fans or lines. The shapes do not stay still, but move and wave in the sky.

Why do they appear?

A thin layer of gas, called the atmosphere, covers our planet Earth. We can't see it, but we know it is there. It is the air that we breathe.

When the Sun shines, a stream of tiny particles flows out to planet Earth. Scientists call this the solar wind.

When the solar wind hits the Earth's atmosphere, it makes flashes of colour in the sky: these are the Northern lights.

Where can you see the Northern lights?

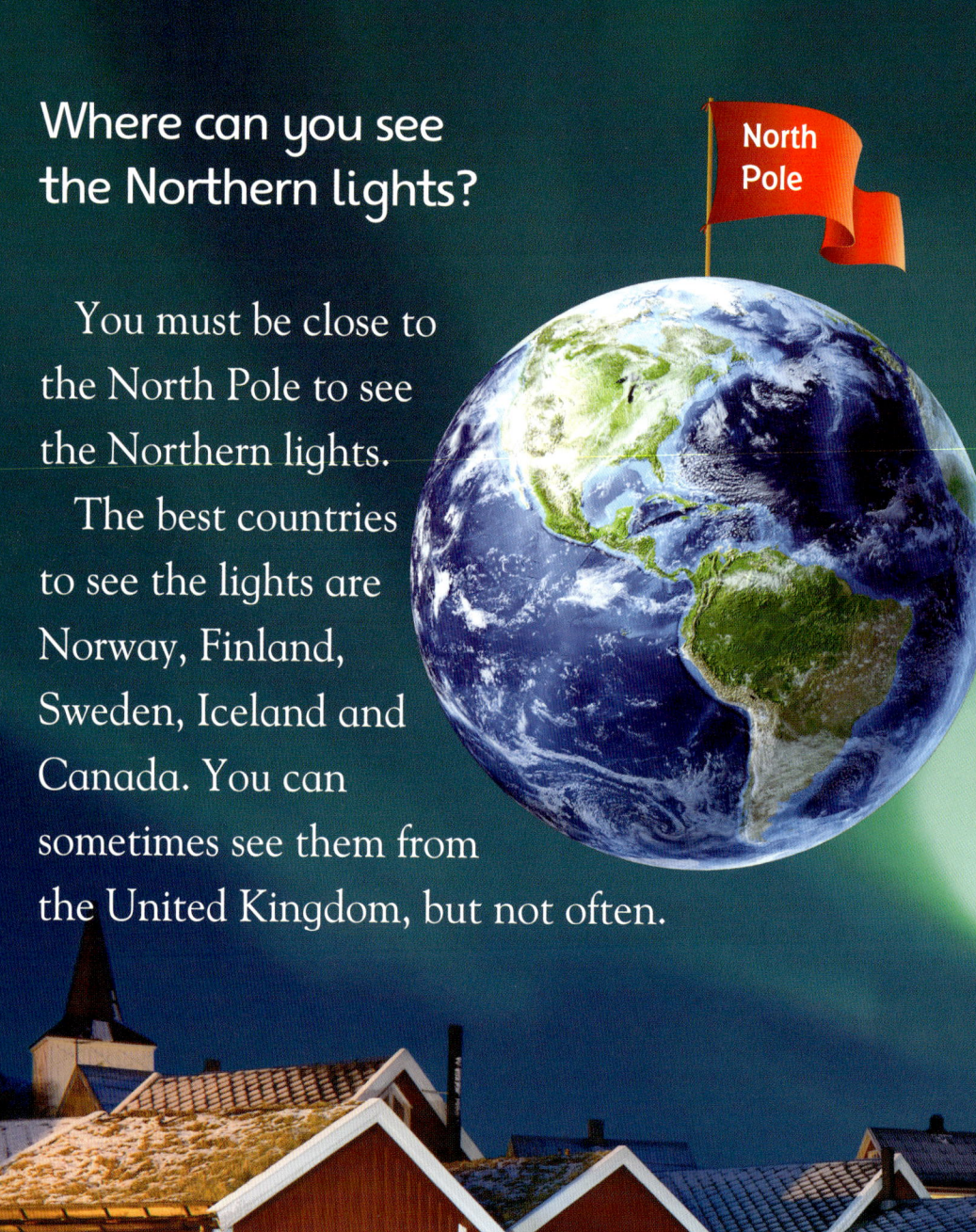

North Pole

You must be close to the North Pole to see the Northern lights.

The best countries to see the lights are Norway, Finland, Sweden, Iceland and Canada. You can sometimes see them from the United Kingdom, but not often.

If you are near the South Pole, you may see the Southern lights. These are just like the Northern lights, but at the other side of the world.

When can you see the Northern lights?

People travel for hundreds of miles to see this beautiful light show, but they are often disappointed. The Northern lights can appear at any time of the year, but they do not appear very often and nobody knows exactly when they will appear.

So you must be in the right place and at the right time to see the Northern lights.

Stories and science

For thousands of years people made up stories about the Northern lights.

Some people thought that they were fires in the sky. Other people thought that they were spirits of the dead.

Now, scientists send rockets into space to find out more about the Northern lights. Now we understand much more about them.

This photograph shows the Northern lights above our planet Earth. The photograph was taken from the International Space Station.

The Northern lights are a beautiful, natural wonder. Most people who look at them still find them magical.